KARL OTTO

Baby Girl

A Novella in Three Parts

Contents

1

Baby Girl

John woke before the alarm. He always did on run days. The house was quiet in the way empty places get when they have learned not to expect anyone back. He moved through it without turning on lights, feet remembering the floorboards better than his eyes ever could.

Coffee. Black. Strong enough to bite.

He drank it standing at the counter, staring at nothing in particular, letting the heat wake the parts of him that still worked.

The '68 Impala waited in the garage. It was older than most of the men who tried to police the roads now. That alone made it useful. No onboard systems. No live telemetry. Nothing that talked back unless it was breaking down.

John liked that. He trusted machines that complained honestly.

He checked the trunk first. Blankets folded tight. Water. Food sealed and rationed. Extra plates wrapped in cloth. Paper maps with pencil marks layered over old routes. Nothing flashy. Nothing sentimental.

The keychain hung from the hook by habit more than necessity. Pink. Plastic worn smooth at the edges. Gold lettering dulled by years of being handled without thought.

BABY GIRL.

John took it down and weighed it in his palm for a moment. Then, with the faint hitch that came when he first put weight on one leg, he slid into the driver's seat and set it in the ignition.

"Long one tonight," he said quietly, to the car or to the space beside him. It didn't matter which.

He adjusted the mirrors, then turned the radio on just long enough to confirm it worked before switching it off again. Silence was safer. Silence let you hear things coming. The engine turned over on the second try. A familiar rumble. Not eager. Willing.

John rested his hands on the wheel and closed his eyes for a breath. "Same rules as always," he murmured. "In and out. No mistakes." The garage door lifted slowly, protesting the cold. Outside, the road waited. Dark. Empty. Patient.

John eased the Impala forward and pulled into the night, already following routes his body remembered even when his mind wandered elsewhere. Somewhere north, two people were waiting.

And John drove, because that was what he did now.

The turnout sat just past a blind curve, gravel cutting away from the road into trees thick enough to block headlights. John rolled in slowly and stopped with the engine still running. He shut off the lights, then shifted in his seat, working the stiffness from one leg before settling again.

Quiet settled in.

A woman stepped out from the tree line and raised a hand. Not a wave. Just checking.

John lifted two fingers from the wheel, then let them fall again.

She came closer. The girl followed a step behind, backpack slung over one shoulder, one hand tight on the strap. The girl slowed when she got a better look at John, her eyes moving from his face to the car.

John rolled the window down. "John," he said.

The woman took him in. The car. The fact that he hadn't asked anything yet.

"You're late." Her tone was cautious.

"Traffic wasn't good."

She let out a short breath. "It never is."

"I'm Ellen. This is Mara."

Mara nodded. No handshake.

"First names only," John said. "That's enough."

Ellen nodded. That seemed to settle something.

John stepped out, favoring one leg just enough to slow the motion, and opened the rear door. Where a seat should have been sat a large, hard-sided cooler bolted to the floor.

"Everything electronic goes in here." His words were short and firm.

Mara frowned. "Like... just phones?"

"Phones. Watches. Anything that connects." John's voice was direct.

Ellen didn't argue. She pulled one phone from her pocket, then another from her bag. Mara hesitated, then unclasped her watch and dropped it in. John watched until they were done.

"Keys are fine," he said.

Mara gave a quiet laugh she hadn't meant to let out. Ellen shot her a look.

John closed the lid and latched it. "If we get separated," he said, "that stays in the car."

Mara swallowed. "Okay."

They got in. Ellen took the back seat, bag at her feet. Mara slid into the front, looking over the dash, the mirrors, the lack of screens.

"You don't use GPS?" she asked.

"No."

"How do you know where you're going?"

John pulled back onto the road. "I've been doing it a while."

They drove a few minutes before Ellen spoke again. "How long is this trip?"

"Two days if nothing goes wrong. Longer if it does."

Mara shifted, and John adjusted his leg against the pedals before settling back into a steadier rhythm. "And if it really goes wrong?"

"Then we deal with it."

Ellen watched him in the mirror. "She just turned eighteen."

John nodded once.

"They started sending letters last year," Ellen said. "Meetings. Programs. Then marriage camp."

Mara stared out the window. "It is optional."

Ellen didn't argue. She just said, "For now."

John kept his eyes on the road.

"At twenty-one," Ellen added, quieter, "it's not optional anymore."

The road climbed. Trees thickened. The signal dropped out. Mara glanced down at her wrist, then back out at the dark.

"When do we stop?" she asked.

John thought for a second. "A couple of hours before daylight. Somewhere quiet."

"Okay."

They drove on. The Impala settled into the climb, engine steady, miles passing whether anyone talked or not.

They stopped just after noon. The gas station sat off a two-lane road that hadn't been repaved in years, the asphalt cracked into long, pale veins. No chain logos. No digital signs. Just pumps that looked older than the Impala and a squat building with sun-faded lettering John didn't bother reading.

He picked the far pump. "Stay close," he said, already stepping out.

Ellen nodded and followed. Mara lingered for a second, stretching her back before getting out, then stayed within arm's reach like she'd been told.

John filled the tank slowly, topping it off all the way. He watched the road more than the numbers. Then the three of them walked to the building.

Inside, the place smelled like burnt coffee and fryer oil. Ellen grabbed water and packaged sandwiches without asking what anyone wanted. Mara stood in front of a rack of trail mix and jerky, turning one bag over, then another.

"This one's stale," she said quietly, holding one up.

"They all are," Ellen said. "Pick the least bad."

A cracked plastic display sat by the register, packed with cheap impulse-buy junk. Lighters. Peppermints. Off-brand sunglasses. Little boxes of miniature troll dolls with wild neon hair sticking up like electrical fires.

Mara stopped and leaned in, squinting at them. "Well, hell," she said.

John glanced over from the coffee machine. "What?"

She pointed through the plastic window of one of the boxes. "That one looks like you."

He stepped closer, favoring one leg just slightly, and looked down. The doll inside had a hard little scowl, thick eyebrows, and a puff of dark hair standing straight up like it had been personally offended by the laws of nature.

John snorted. "That thing looks like it bites children."

"Exactly," Mara said. "It's you."

Ellen looked over from the next aisle, took one glance, and laughed into her sleeve.

John shook his head and reached for the coffee. "Get your snacks."

Mara grinned, but lingered a second longer, studying the little box like she was filing it away for later.

Then she trotted off toward the chips.

John paid cash. The clerk didn't look at them long enough to remember their faces.

Outside, Ellen handed out the food without ceremony. They ate standing up, leaning against the car. Nobody said much. The sandwiches were dry. The water was warm.

Mara watched a pickup roll past on the road. She didn't say anything until it was gone. "How much farther today?" she asked.

John wiped his hands on a rag and folded it back into his pocket. "Till after dark."

"That could mean anything."

"It does."

She nodded, accepting that.

When they pulled back onto the road, clouds were starting to gather over the ridgeline. The light flattened, losing its edge. A few miles later, rain began to spot the windshield, light at first, then steady.

John turned the wipers on low.

Ellen closed her eyes. Not sleep exactly. Just rest.

Mara watched the rain run down the windshield, the trees beyond it blurring as the road narrowed again through the climb.

The miles kept coming.

They pulled off the road just after midnight.

John took the turn without slowing, tires crunching over gravel and leaf litter until the trees swallowed the car. He killed the engine and let the Impala roll the last few feet on momentum alone. When it stopped, he shifted once in his seat before getting out, working the stiffness from one leg. The dark settled back in around them like it had never been disturbed.

"This is it," he said.

The campsite was small. A clearing cut just wide enough for a car and a tent, the Appalachian Trail running close enough that you could feel it even if you couldn't see it. No fire ring. No sign. Just ground flattened by years of people who knew better than to leave traces.

A narrow side trail cut off from the clearing, barely visible unless you knew what to look for. A faded blue rectangular blaze marked the tree at its mouth.

Someone stood just beyond it.

He was half in shadow, his pack set down at his feet, his body angled like he'd been there long enough to choose the best place to disappear from. Older. Beard gone to gray in uneven patches. He didn't step forward or raise his hands. He just watched.

John nodded once.

The man tilted his head, then gave a small smile.

"I thought you gave this up," he said.

"This is my last run," John replied.

The man's eyes flicked to the Impala, then back. "She's still running good?"

"Good enough."

He huffed a quiet laugh. "That old thing ain't never going to die."

Ellen and Mara had gotten out by then, staying close without being told. Ellen watched carefully. Mara's gaze moved between the two men, sensing the shape of something she didn't yet understand.

The man shifted his weight. "Long day?"

"Long road," John said.

"That tracks."

They stood there a moment longer than necessary.

"Good to see you, Baby Girl," the man said.

Mara blinked.

John didn't react. "You too, Cold Camp."

That was it.

John turned to Ellen and Mara. "He's fine."

Ellen accepted it immediately. Mara hesitated, then nodded, trusting the certainty in John's voice more than the situation itself.

Cold Camp glanced at the car again. "You carrying anything fresh?"

John considered it for half a second, then popped the trunk.

He handed over a loaf of bread wrapped in paper, two apples with the shine still on them, and a strip of jerky that hadn't yet dried into dust.

Cold Camp took them without ceremony, weighing the apples in his hands like he was relearning their shape.

"I got blueberry," he said.

John nodded. He knew better than to ask for fruit.

Cold Camp reached into his pack and produced a small mason jar, cloudy and pale in the low light.

"Fair trade," he added.

"Fair," John said.

They didn't shake on it. They didn't need to.

Cold Camp stepped back toward the blue-marked trail. "Flat ground's yours," he said. "Trail's been quiet. Your handoff is Mama Desh."

"Well, at least that's good news."

They settled in without ceremony. No tent. Just blankets laid out in the back of the car, windows cracked enough to keep the air moving. John checked the perimeter once, more out of habit than fear.

Cold Camp lingered a moment longer, then faded back toward the trees, his presence dissolving as naturally as it had appeared.

John sat on the rear bumper and unscrewed the jar. The sharp, sweet smell of homemade liquor rose at once, biting through the night air.

Mara appeared a moment later, arms folded tight against herself, shoulders hunched as the cold crept in. "That smells like paint thinner."

"That," John said, "is the smell of craftsmanship."

"It smells like something you siphon out of a tractor."

Ellen took the jar when he handed it over, swallowed, coughed once, then handed it back with watering eyes. "Sweet Jesus."

John took a pull of his own and felt the burn hit all the way down. For a second, that was enough. Cold air. Contraband liquor. The engine ticking as it cooled. No sirens. No uniforms. No one asking for papers.

For a few minutes, they sat without talking. Just the night, the trees, the sound of water moving somewhere out of sight.

"Baby Girl," Mara said softly. "That's... the car?"

John looked at the hood, dull with road dust.

"Yeah," he said. "It's her trail name."

He rubbed the fender absently, like checking that something was still there.

"Ain't that right, Baby Girl?"

Mara didn't say anything. She just smiled, small and warm, like she'd been let in on something without needing it explained.

Then she rubbed her hands up and down her arms.

John noticed without thinking. He pushed himself up, slower on one side, set the jar on the ground, and turned back to the trunk. He dug under a canvas bag until he found the old blanket stuffed in the corner. Faded brown. Thin in places, but warm enough.

He held it out to her.

Mara blinked. "What's that?"

"A blanket," he said. "You planning to freeze on principle?"

She took it slowly, like she hadn't expected the offer to be real. "Oh."

"Don't make it weird."

That pulled the ghost of a smile out of her. She wrapped it around her shoulders, tucked her hands under the edge, and sank down onto the tailgate beside the jar. Ellen settled next to her, hip to hip, stealing a little of the blanket without asking.

"Rude," Mara muttered.

"Be respectful to your elders," Ellen said.

John reached for the jar again while Mara began digging around in the pocket of her hoodie with the hand that wasn't clutching the blanket closed.

"What now?" he said.

She pulled out something small and plastic, then another, then another, and held them in her palm like contraband treasure.

John squinted. "Are those troll dolls?"

Mara looked offended. "Mini troll dolls."

Ellen leaned in, then barked out a tired laugh. "You bought them?"

Mara shrugged, suddenly looking younger than she had all day. "They looked like they wanted to come with me."

"Pretty sure that's how stores work," John said.

She ignored him and held one up. It had wild dark hair standing straight up and a tiny molded face that looked deeply unimpressed with existence.

Mara pointed it at John. "It looks exactly like you."

Ellen laughed harder this time, covering her mouth.

John looked at the doll in the dim moonlight. Thick little eyebrows. A hard scowl. Hair like it had been electrocuted by spite.

"I do not look like this."

"You absolutely do," Mara said.

"No, he does," Ellen said. "That is Tiny John."

John looked from one to the other, then back at the doll. "This thing looks like it bites people."

"Only if they deserve it," Mara said.

She picked out another one and handed it to Ellen. Bright orange hair. Big vacant grin. Ellen accepted it on principle.

Then Mara held out the third one to John.

He looked at it for a second, then at her.

"Go on," she said. "You're one of us now."

Something in the words caught.

Not enough to name. Just a small, strange hitch somewhere under his ribs, quick and sharp as a hook.

John took the doll.

For a second, he only stood there, his thumb resting against the cheap plastic face while the fire snapped in the distance and the night pressed in around the camp.

Then he cleared his throat.

"Well," he said, tucking the thing into his coat pocket, "that's the stupidest initiation ritual I ever saw."

Mara grinned and pulled the blanket tighter around herself.

"Still counts."

John picked up the jar and took another swallow, harsher this time. When he handed it off, he didn't look at either of them. He just leaned back against the Impala, listening to the engine tick and the low murmur of strangers in the dark, with the tiny troll doll sitting warm and ridiculous in his pocket.

For the first time in a long while, the night felt a little less empty.

John turned away first.

Clouds slid across the moon, breaking the light into uneven pieces. The night held.

John didn't sleep much. He rarely did on the first night.

Before dawn, Cold Camp was gone.

No goodbye. No sign he had ever been there.

John started the engine softly.

The road waited.

They were back on the road before the sky had fully made up its mind.

The light came slow and gray, filtering through low clouds that clung to the ridgelines. The mountains felt closer in daylight, not smaller. Like they were watching more carefully.

They drove north on roads that bent when they felt like it. Switchbacks, long climbs, descents that made Ellen grip the door handle without realizing she was doing it. John drove steady and unhurried, adjusting his leg once on the pedals when the grade changed. The Impala knew these grades, or close enough.

Mara dozed in the passenger seat, waking only when the road surface changed or the gears shifted rough. Ellen stayed awake, eyes forward, taking in the land like she was trying to memorize it.

After an hour, the traffic picked up. Not much. Just enough to notice. Old vans. Cars with gear strapped where luggage should have been. Packs visible through back windows. People who weren't in a hurry to get anywhere.

Ellen frowned. "What's going on up here?"

John kept his eyes on the road. "Trail Days."

She glanced at him. "What's that?"

"Hiking festival," he said. "Once a year. Folks come off the Appalachian Trail. People who aren't on it yet. People who never leave it. Town fills up."

"That seems... random."

"Only if you're not part of it."

Mara stirred. "Is that bad?"

"It's busy," John said. "Busy can be useful."

The town came into view in pieces. Handwritten signs tacked to fences. Arrows that pointed to places that weren't on any map. The road narrowed, then widened again to accommodate vehicles that had no intention of going anywhere fast.

People crossed without looking. Packs brushed bumpers. Dogs on improvised leashes. Conversations stacked on top of each other, none of them meant to last.

Music drifted from somewhere deeper in town. Laughter. Someone shouting about food. The sound of too many bodies sharing too little space.

"This might actually help," Ellen said, tentative.

"It doesn't hurt," John replied. He didn't say more.

He found a place to park that wasn't marked and probably wasn't meant for it. He killed the engine and waited a beat before moving.

"We get what we need and we leave," he said. "No browsing."

They split up without ceremony.

John pulled a ball cap from the glove box and settled it low before heading into the auto parts store. Inside, the air was cool and smelled faintly of rubber and oil. He kept his head down, angled just enough that the brim shadowed his face when he passed beneath the security cameras.

He moved like he belonged there. Grabbed what he needed. Paid cash. Didn't rush.

Outside, the noise felt louder. Sharper.

A group of hikers stood in the middle of the street arguing about nothing in particular. Someone strummed a guitar badly. A man with a megaphone shouted about free meals and missing dogs.

John checked his watch.

He stepped back onto the sidewalk, eyes scanning for Ellen and Mara.

That was when he saw the uniforms.

They didn't look like they belonged. Clean. Calculated in their movements. Standing where people naturally flowed around them like rocks in a stream.

Ellen was just ahead of them.

She hadn't noticed yet.

John started forward, favoring one side just enough to throw a hitch into his first step.

It happened fast.

Not rushed. Not sloppy. Just fast in the way practiced things are.

Ellen felt it before she understood it.

The space around her tightened. A shadow where there hadn't been one a second before. She turned and found a man standing close enough that she had to step back to see his face.

Another was already there.

Her breath caught.

"I..." she started, then stopped. Her hand came up without thinking, fingers curling into the strap of her bag like it might anchor her to the ground.

"Ma'am," one of them said, calm and flat. "We need you to come with us."

Her heart kicked hard against her ribs.

"Why?" she asked. The word came out thin as she tried to sound confident.

The second man shifted, just slightly, putting his body between her and the street. Blocking angles. Closing exits.

Ellen looked past them, eyes searching until they landed on Mara.

"Mara," she said, sharp with fear now. "Mara, don't..."

Mara stepped forward instinctively.

John moved at the same time.

He caught Mara by the arm and pulled her back hard, dragging her into the shadow of the storefront. She stumbled, the breath knocked out of her.

"Don't," he said, low and urgent. "Look at me."

She fought him for a second, panic flashing across her face, then stilled when she saw his eyes. Not calm. Focused. Unnervingly settled.

Ellen saw it.

Her chest tightened. She shook her head once, small and desperate.

"I haven't done anything," she said to the men, her voice trembling now. "Please. We're just..."

"I can explain," one of them said. "Just not here."

"No," Ellen said. The word came out before she could stop it. "Please. She's just a kid."

A hiker nearby stopped walking. Someone else turned. A voice from the crowd said, "Hey."

The attention made Ellen's breathing go shallow. She could feel it slipping. Control. The moment.

The second man took her wrist.

She flinched hard.

"Don't touch me," she said, louder than she meant to. "Please."

The grip tightened. Not painful. Not gentle. Final.

"Now," he said.

Mara made a sound that John felt in his chest.

Ellen looked at her one last time. Fear, naked and unguarded.

"Take care of her," she mouthed. Not brave. Not composed. Just terrified and trying to do one last thing right.

Then they turned her.

The crowd pressed closer. Someone shouted. Someone else stepped forward and was shoved aside without ceremony. Phones came up, then went down again.

The agents moved Ellen with practiced efficiency, guiding her through bodies toward a vehicle she hadn't noticed until it was right there. The door opened.

She resisted then. Just a step. A hand braced against the frame.

"Please," she said again. "Please."

The door closed.

It was done.

The vehicle pulled away.

The crowd surged and then broke apart, noise spilling everywhere now that there was nothing left to stop it. Arguments flared. Someone yelled at no one in particular.

John held Mara as she shook.

"She didn't do anything," Mara whispered. "She didn't…"

"I know," John said.

He didn't let go until the street swallowed the place where Ellen had been.

They didn't speak until they were out of town.

John drove like the road might vanish if he stopped paying attention to it. Turn after turn, back into hills that didn't care what had happened a few miles south. The noise of Trail Days faded quickly, swallowed by trees and distance.

Mara sat rigid in the passenger seat, arms folded tight across her chest. Her breathing came shallow and fast, like she was afraid to let too much air in at once.

"She didn't do anything," she said again.

"I know."

"You saw it. You were right there."

"I know."

Her jaw tightened. She looked out the window, then back at him. "Then why didn't you do something?"

John didn't answer right away.

The road narrowed. He slowed without thinking, easing his leg as he let a pickup pass in the opposite direction before settling back into the lane.

"What was I supposed to do?" Mara pressed. "Just stand there?"

"No," he said. "You were supposed to stay alive."

She laughed, sharp and ugly. "That's it? That's the plan?"

"That's the plan."

She shook her head, eyes bright now. "You grabbed me. You dragged me away. You didn't even..."

"I did exactly what I needed to do."

"For who?" she snapped.

John kept his eyes forward. "For you."

"That wasn't your call."

"It was."

Silence slammed down between them.

Mara turned toward the window again, shoulders shaking now, breath hitching in ways she couldn't control. She wiped her face hard with the heel of her hand, angry at the tears as much as the situation. "You don't get to decide that," she said, quieter. "You don't get to decide who gets taken."

John swallowed. "I don't," he said. "But I know how this ends when people try to stop it."

She laughed again, hollow. "So you just let it happen."

"No," he said. "I planned for it."

That landed differently.

She looked at him then, really looked. "You knew this could happen."

"Yes."

"And you still brought us here."

"Yes."

Her mouth opened. Closed. She shook her head slowly, like she was trying to reset something inside herself.

"I trusted you," she said.

John nodded once. "You still should."

"Why?"

Because he'd been here before. Because he knew the shape of what came next. Because the people who survived were the ones who kept moving.

None of that felt like an answer that wouldn't break her.

"Because you're still here," he said instead.

She turned away.

They drove for another hour before she spoke again.

"Where are we going now?"

John adjusted the mirror, checking the road behind them.

"North," he said.

"And my aunt?"

He didn't answer.

She nodded like she'd expected that.

The Impala climbed, engine steady, carrying two people who no longer agreed on what survival meant.

The road didn't care.

They drove long after dark.

The road narrowed again, climbing into colder air. Trees pressed close, the headlights carving a thin tunnel that never seemed to widen. John drove with one hand on the wheel, the other resting near the ignition, his thumb brushing the edge of the keychain without looking at it.

Mara sat quiet beside him. Too quiet.

After a while, her breathing changed. Slowed. Evened out. She let her head tip toward the window, eyes closed just enough to sell it. John noticed. He always noticed. He didn't say anything.

The radio stayed off.

Miles passed.

John spoke softly, not to Mara, not to himself.

"I couldn't stop it."

Mara's breath hitched, almost imperceptibly. She kept her eyes closed.

"They do it fast now," he continued. "They don't give you time to think. That's on purpose."

He paused, shifting his leg once under the dash before swallowing.

"I saw it coming," he said. "That part's on me."

The road curved. The Impala leaned into it, steady and sure.

"She was scared," John said. "Tried to be brave anyway. That's how they get you."

His hand tightened on the wheel. Not angry. Controlled.

"I kept the kid back. That's what mattered. That's what you'd have wanted."

Another pause.

"I know," he said quietly. "I know it doesn't make it right."

Mara's chest felt tight. She focused on the rhythm of the tires, the rise and fall of the road, anything that wasn't his voice.

John exhaled through his nose.

"I don't tell them," he went on. "The people I move. I don't tell them what it's really like. I just tell them where to sit and when to keep quiet."

The keychain tapped softly against the dash as the car shifted.

"They think I'm calm," he said. "They think I've got a plan."

He let out a breath that might once have been a laugh.

"I do. Just not the kind they want."

Silence again.

Then, quieter still.

"I didn't freeze. I didn't run. I didn't look away."

His voice roughened, just a little.

"I just... did the thing that lets me keep going."

The road straightened. The trees thinned briefly, revealing a stretch of sky dusted with stars.

"I'm sorry," he said. Not to Mara. Not to Ellen. "I'm sorry I keep choosing the road."

Mara opened her eyes then.

She didn't turn toward him. Didn't move at all. She stared straight ahead, heart pounding, the pieces sliding into place with awful clarity.

The trail name.

The way he talked to the car.

The rules.

The planning.

This wasn't new for him.

This was grief with a route map.

John cleared his throat and rubbed the dashboard once, absently.

"We'll get her as far as we can," he said. "Then I'll turn around."

The car hummed beneath them, eating miles, carrying two people bound together by something neither of them had asked for.

Mara said nothing.

But she didn't pretend to sleep again.

They crossed into colder country before dawn.

The trees changed first. Thinner. Straighter. The kind that let wind through instead of blocking it. The road followed suit, longer stretches without turns, fewer places to pull off without being seen.

Mara watched the signs as they passed. County names she didn't recognize. Distances that felt both too long and not long enough.

John stopped once to refuel. He didn't turn the engine off. Didn't go inside. He paid through the slot and took the change without comment. Mara stayed in the car, hands folded in her lap, eyes on the mirrors.

When they were back on the road, she said, "You ever get tired?"

He nodded. "Yeah."

"That doesn't stop you."

"No."

She waited a beat. "Why?"

John thought about it longer than he had to.

"Because stopping isn't doing anything," he said. "And I used to do a lot of nothing."

The words sat between them.

The sky stayed low and gray. A fine mist settled in, enough to keep the wipers going but not enough to wash anything clean. The Impala pressed on, engine steady but working harder now, climbing grades John didn't know as well.

His shoulders ached. His eyes burned. He flexed his fingers at red lights that lasted too long.

Mara noticed.

"You want me to drive?" she asked.

He shook his head. "Not yet."

"Later?"

"Maybe."

That was more than he usually offered.

They ate cold food without talking. Took turns watching the road when the other blinked too long. When they stopped to stretch, neither went more than a few steps from the car.

By midafternoon, the land flattened briefly, then rose again, sharper this time. Snow clung to the shadows, old and dirty, refusing to melt.

Mara pulled her jacket tighter. "Is it always like this up here?"

"No," John said. "Sometimes it's worse."

She smiled faintly at that.

They drove until the light started to fail again.

The road narrowed. The shoulders disappeared. John slowed, his jaw tight now, his focus sharpened by fatigue.

"We'll stop soon," he said. "Short one."

She nodded. "Okay."

There was no argument this time.

As the car climbed, Mara rested her head against the seat and watched the keychain sway with each turn.

Baby Girl.

She didn't ask about it again.

John kept driving, carrying them north, knowing exactly how much farther he could push before the road demanded something back.

They reached the place just after dark.

Not a border. Not yet. Just one of the seams where roads lost their names and directions stopped meaning much. A narrow pull-off cut into the trees, barely wide enough for two cars if they trusted each other not to move.

John didn't.

He parked at an angle, nose pointed back the way they'd come. Left the engine running.

"There," he said. "This is it."

Mara sat up straighter. "This doesn't look like anything."

"That's the idea."

Headlights appeared through the trees a minute later. Slow. Careful. An older sedan rolled in and stopped a respectful distance away.

A woman stepped out.

She was older. Seventies, maybe more. Her hair was pulled back, streaked white but thick. She moved with purpose, not haste. Someone who knew exactly where her body was in the dark.

She didn't look surprised to see Mara.

"Come here, sweetheart," the woman said, her voice warm and steady. Not loud. Not whispered. Certain.

Mara hesitated, then stepped out of the Impala.

John popped the cooler.

He handed Mara her phone first. Then her watch. Then another phone. And another.

She frowned, confused, until she recognized them.

Her aunt's.

The weight of them hit harder than she expected. Not heavy in her hands. Heavy in what they meant. Messages that would never be sent. Calls that would never be answered. Proof that Ellen hadn't planned on disappearing. She had planned on making it the whole way.

Mara swallowed and tucked them carefully into her bag.

John didn't say anything. He just waited.

The older woman stayed where she was, patient, giving Mara the space to decide how long she needed.

Mara took two steps toward her, then stopped and turned back.

Before John could say anything, she leaned in and hugged him. Quick. Hard. The kind of hug that was over before you could think about it.

"Thank you," she said into his shoulder.

He froze for half a beat, then rested a hand lightly against her back.

"You're going to be okay," he said.

She pulled back.

He looked at her face, really looked, and the name slipped out before he could stop it.

"Em..."

He cut himself off.

Mara didn't react. She didn't know the name, didn't need to. She just nodded once, like she understood the feeling even if she didn't know the source.

The older woman stepped closer, placing a hand gently at Mara's elbow.

"I've got her," she said to John. Not a statement. A promise.

John nodded.

They didn't shake hands.

Mara took one last look at the Impala, at the keychain swaying faintly in the ignition, then let herself be guided toward the other car.

The door closed softly.

The sedan pulled away, its lights swallowed by trees and distance.

John sat there longer than necessary, the engine humming beneath him.

Then he turned the car around.

South.

John pulled off the road long enough to write.

He didn't kill the engine. He just shifted into park and let the headlights wash over the trees while he opened the notebook on his knee. The pages were thin, curled at the edges, filled with the same careful hand.

Tomorrow.

0400.

West of Mill Creek.

Two names.

One kid.

He underlined the time once, closed the notebook, and slid it back into the door pocket where he could reach it without looking.

The road was quiet. The kind of quiet that let memories slip in if you weren't careful.

He rested his hands on the wheel.

And there it was.

Emily stood at the edge of the driveway, arms folded, trying not to look tired.

She was paler. Enough that he noticed. Enough that it scared him more than he let on.

"You don't have to hover," she said. "I'm not made of glass."

"I know," John replied. "Glass is easier to replace."

She rolled her eyes. "You're impossible."

The Impala sat behind her, freshly washed and ready. He'd done it himself. Didn't trust anyone else to.

He reached into his pocket and pulled out the keychain.

Pink. Cheap. The letters bright.

BABY GIRL.

Emily stared at it. Then laughed. "You're kidding."

"Nope."

"Dad."

He threaded the keys through it slowly, deliberately, like the motion mattered.

"Why Baby Girl?" she asked.

He didn't hesitate. "Because that's what you are. My baby girl."

She blinked, caught off guard despite herself, then scoffed to cover it. "That's corny."

"It's accurate."

He held the keys out to her.

She took them, turning the keychain over in her fingers, letting it swing. "So I get the car now?"

He smiled warmly. "Yes, you do, Baby Girl."

She grinned. "I knew it. You're finally admitting I'm responsible."

His eyes widened slightly, and he snagged the keys back immediately.

"I don't know what I was thinking," he said. "You're not driving to Illinois tomorrow."

Her smile faltered. "What?"

"I am," he said. "You get to sit. Hydrate. Pretend you're not exhausted."

She frowned. "I feel fine."

"You are sick and stubborn," he said, "which is not a license."

She laughed despite herself. "You're really not letting me drive at all?"

"Absolutely not," he said. "You can drive us home. If you're still feeling good. And if I'm dead tired. And if the world's feeling generous."

"So... no."

"Correct."

She stepped forward and hugged him, careful but fierce.

"Thanks, Dad," she said. "For the car. And everything else."

He rested his chin on the top of her head for half a second longer than necessary.

"We'll get there," he said. "Then we'll get you better."

She nodded into his shoulder. "Okay."

John opened his eyes.

The Impala sat quiet around him, engine humming low. The keychain hung from the ignition, worn smooth now, the gold lettering dulled by years of being touched without thought.

BABY GIRL.

"Yeah," he said softly, rubbing the dash once. "I know."

He reached for the notebook, checked the time, then pulled back onto the road.

There was always another pickup.

And John drove.

2

Polling Place 12

November 2028 — Jacksonville, Florida

The garage was cool and damp, the kind of Florida morning that settled into the skin without making a case for itself. Moisture clung to the concrete and the metal shelving alike, leaving everything faintly slick, as if the air had passed through while he slept and rearranged things.

John left the door half open. Gray light slid in low and flat, stopping short of the Impala's tires. Somewhere down the block, a car tried to turn over and failed. Then the neighborhood went quiet again.

The '68 Impala waited.

He didn't bother with the overhead light. He knew the space by feel. The workbench was where it always was, the rag folded at the edge, clean enough to feel out of place. He picked it up, turned it once in his hands, then drew it across the hood in slow, even passes. Not polishing. Just clearing the night off.

Dust came away in pale streaks. He stopped there.

The keychain hung by the door, pink plastic dulled and chipped. He took it down and let it swing once before closing his hand around it. The letters pressed unevenly into his palm.

BABY GIRL.

The back door groaned as he opened it. The rear seat caught his eye immediately, not because of how it looked, but because of how it didn't match the rest of the interior anymore. The leather there had lost something. Not color exactly. Response. It no longer caught the light the same way the front seats did.

John stood with one hand on the doorframe, looking at the seat without focusing on it. His thumb brushed the surface once, paused, then moved on.

The quilt sat folded on the bench. He lifted it, set it back down, then picked it up again and carried it to the car. The fabric spread across the seat easily, corners tucked in with care. He stopped short of smoothing it flat, leaving a faint ridge where the leather dipped beneath.

Close enough.

He stepped back and let the back door swing shut.

The trunk opened with a hollow sound. He laid everything out in a line on the concrete. Bottled water sweating despite the hour. Wrapped snacks. The first aid kit, its zipper catching before giving way. He tugged it closed, then opened it again and checked the contents by touch.

Bandages. Gloves. Antiseptic.

He closed the trunk and pressed down until it latched. Pressed again.

His hands stayed there longer than necessary.

He slipped the keys into his pocket.

The driver's door complained when he opened it. He paused, then slid into the seat anyway. The leather held the night longer than the air had, cool against his back. He adjusted the seat forward, then back. The mirror caught his face for a moment before he nudged it aside.

The engine turned over on the second try. It settled into a low, steady idle. John rested his hands on the wheel and waited until the faint tremor in his fingers passed.

He backed out slowly. The garage door rolled down behind him.

Out on the road, the Impala smoothed out as it warmed. Palm fronds stirred overhead, dark against a sky just beginning to lift. Houses slid past, windows still dark.

The pickup point was a few miles away. John followed the route by memory, eyes forward.

The road stretched ahead, long and flat.

John stayed with it and drove.

John reached the pickup point ten minutes early and cut the engine as soon as he pulled in. The lot sat behind a low brick church that hadn't opened its doors yet, the sign out front still advertising last week's food pantry hours. A few cars were already there, parked with the casual imprecision of people who hadn't planned to stay long.

No one stood in a line.

They leaned against fenders, sat on the low retaining wall, pretended to scroll through phones that weren't connected to anything. A woman smoked half a cigarette and crushed it out with her shoe, then stayed where she was. When the Impala pulled in, the space adjusted around it. Not attention exactly. Orientation.

John stayed in the driver's seat, hands resting on the wheel as he watched how no one looked directly at the car for more than a second. He took that as permission and stepped out.

A man near the wall straightened and gave a small nod. Another person glanced past John toward the back seat, then away again.

"You're the one she mentioned," the older woman said. She held a plastic folder against her chest, edges worn thin from handling.

John inclined his head. He didn't correct her.

The idea had come to him weeks earlier, sitting across from a friend he knew through the Crescent & Field Network, someone whose work was focused on preparedness rather than response. Not an official suggestion. Just something he'd said out loud. What if rides were the missing piece?

The answer hadn't been framed as approval or refusal.

Some people could use help.

He opened the back door first, giving them time to look inside. The quilt stayed where it was, folded neatly across the seat. No one commented on it.

They moved in without being directed. The older woman settled carefully, placing the folder on her lap. A younger man followed, phone still in his hand, gaze shifting between John and the lot. A third person paused, fingers tightening on the door handle.

"You can do this. We'll be okay," John said.

The pause stretched, then broke. The door closed.

Once everyone was inside, John walked back around and took the driver's seat. He waited for the small sounds to finish: seatbelts finding their locks, fabric adjusting, breath redistributing in the confined space.

"Couple things," he said. "We stay together. If something feels off, we come back to the car. No arguing with anyone in a uniform. I'll handle that."

Heads nodded.

He started the engine. In the rearview mirror, he saw the passengers take one last look at the lot.

They pulled out quietly, merging with the thin early traffic. The church slipped behind them, then the street, then the neighborhood itself.

John checked the mirrors again, tracking how the idea behaved now that it was moving.

Everyone in the car had chosen this.

He drove.

Traffic thickened as they moved north, not with urgency but with accumulation. Morning commuters slid in and out of lanes with the practiced impatience of people already behind schedule. John kept the Impala steady, neither leading nor lagging, letting the car become one more shape in the flow.

The city came apart in pieces. Strip malls gave way to longer stretches of road. Billboards rose and fell, advertising services meant to solve problems that hadn't been named yet. John clocked exits as they passed them, noting which ones thinned out and which ones didn't. He avoided the highways without consciously deciding to. Surface streets gave him more time.

In the rearview mirror, the passengers watched the world move past the windows. The older woman kept one hand on her folder, thumb pressed along the edge as if counting pages without opening it. The younger man shifted in his seat, phone dark now, screen smudged from earlier handling. No one spoke.

John adjusted the air slightly when he noticed shallow breathing from the back seat. He didn't comment on it. He didn't ask questions that would invite answers he couldn't act on yet.

They passed a school zone marked with fresh paint and portable signs. A crossing guard stood waiting, arms folded, nowhere near any children. The uniform looked official enough. John noted it and moved on.

A police cruiser rolled by in the opposite lane. Then another. Both unhurried. Both indistinguishable from routine. John felt his shoulders tighten and made himself release them again.

The car filled with small, incidental sounds. Turn signals clicking. The low rush of air through a vent. Someone in the back seat adjusting their jacket. Each noise registered and faded.

They approached the polling place from the side streets first. The building appeared in fragments before it was clear: the roofline above trees, a cluster of cars parked where they didn't quite belong, a temporary sign staked into the grass with lettering meant to be legible from a moving vehicle.

Polling Place 12.

The sign didn't point directly at the entrance. It gestured. John followed the direction and slowed as the street narrowed.

People were already there.

Not crowded. Not sparse. Enough to suggest momentum. Enough to make turning back feel noticeable.

John pulled into a stretch of curb a short walk from the entrance and brought the car to a stop. He didn't cut the engine right away. He watched how people moved, how they queued without lining up, how they oriented themselves toward the doors as if pulled by something just inside.

No uniforms in sight.

Phones were out. Conversations overlapped and broke apart. Someone laughed, then covered it quickly. A volunteer adjusted a stack of folded chairs near the entrance and moved them again when they didn't look right.

John made a decision and parked.

He chose a spot close enough that the car stayed in view of the line, far enough that it didn't announce itself as part of the operation. He checked the mirrors, then the street, then the building again. Nothing challenged the choice.

He turned the engine off.

The sudden quiet felt louder than the traffic had. He shifted in his seat and looked back.

"This is it," he said. "We walk together."

The older woman nodded and reached for her folder. The younger man took a breath and let it out slowly. The third passenger watched the entrance without blinking.

John stepped out first and waited while the others followed. He didn't rush them. He didn't hover. He stayed close enough to be part of the group without leading it.

As they moved toward the line, John glanced back at the Impala. The car sat where he'd left it, unremarkable among the others. The quilt was just visible through the rear window, catching the light differently than the rest of the interior.

He turned away.

They took their place at the edge of the gathering. The line absorbed them without comment. A volunteer handed out pamphlets that no one read. A man farther up adjusted his cap and checked his watch.

Time stretched into something measured by foot shuffles and weight shifts.

John stayed with them, eyes moving, taking inventory. Doors. Windows. Paths in and out. He noted where the sidewalk narrowed and where it opened again. He registered how long it took for each person ahead of them to disappear inside and how long it took before the next one moved forward.

Everything still fit the shape he'd planned for.

For now.

The entrance to Polling Place 12 looked temporary even as it asserted itself. A pair of folding tables had been set up just inside the doors, their metal legs capped with rubber feet that squeaked faintly against the tile whenever someone shifted them. Signs taped to the walls pointed in directions that felt provisional, arrows layered over older arrows that had been peeled away and replaced.

John took this in as they stepped forward. Not as threat. As pattern.

A volunteer stood near the doors, vest too clean, smile already in place. She gestured people forward in small groups, spacing them without saying the reason. Her movements were efficient, practiced in a way that suggested rehearsal rather than habit.

The line advanced in short increments. Each step forward felt earned, the result of waiting rather than movement. Conversation thinned as they got closer to the entrance. Phones went dark, then disappeared into pockets. The older woman adjusted her grip on the folder, shifting it from one arm to the other.

Inside, the air changed. Cooler. Filtered. The sound dampened as soon as the doors closed behind them, the noise of the street replaced by the soft overlap of voices and the scrape of shoes on tile. A hand-lettered sign announced the precinct number in block letters.

Polling Place 12.

No uniforms yet. No security.

John registered this immediately. He noted where people stood, where they didn't. He clocked the positions of the tables, the spacing between them, the way the room funneled bodies toward a single point before widening again. He tracked exits without turning his head, counting doorways by reflection and peripheral glance.

The group stayed together as they'd agreed, close enough to share space without clustering. The younger man leaned forward slightly, eyes fixed on the table ahead. The third passenger shifted weight from foot to foot, then stilled.

A staffer behind the first table asked for identification. The request landed gently, framed as routine. Hands moved. Wallets opened. Cards were placed on the table and slid back again.

Everything moved.

John watched faces more than actions. The small tells. The tightening around eyes. The way people exhaled after their documents were returned. The absence of raised voices made the room feel controlled rather than calm.

Someone ahead of them stepped aside at a quiet instruction and was directed toward a secondary table set farther back. The redirection was efficient, almost polite. No explanation followed. The line closed the gap without comment.

John marked the secondary table and adjusted his stance so he could see it clearly. He noticed how the volunteer's smile never changed, even as her attention sharpened.

Still no uniforms. Not even one officer.

He felt the plan hold, but stretched across more variables than he'd accounted for. The group remained intact. The door behind them stayed closed.

John stayed where he was and waited for the next instruction to surface.

The line moved again, this time in smaller increments. Not forward so much as sideways, bodies redirected by subtle gestures that carried the authority of repetition. A staffer lifted a hand and two people peeled off without argument, guided toward the secondary table John had noted of earlier.

Nothing about the movement raised voices. The sounds in the room stayed level. Shoes on tile. Paper sliding across plastic. Quite answers to questions. The calm had structure now.

Identification was requested a second time.

Not from everyone. Only from some.

The older woman stepped forward when her turn came and placed her folder on the table. The staffer opened it without asking, flipping through the contents with a practiced thumb. The motion was quick, almost bored. A pause followed that lasted half a beat longer than the others.

The staffer glanced at a screen, then at the card in her hand. She didn't look up.

A question was asked, phrased as clarification rather than challenge. The older woman answered without hesitation. Another pause. The folder was closed and slid back across the table.

"Please step to the side for a moment."

The request carried weight and didn't need reinforcement.

The line closed in behind her.

John felt the group compress instinctively, the remaining passengers adjusting their spacing without being told. He shifted his stance to keep the older woman within sight as she was guided toward the secondary table. No one else followed her.

At the second table, the process repeated itself with slight variations. Documents were requested again. A different screen. A different staffer. The same bored tone.

John watched how time behaved there. How it slowed without stopping. How the room continued to function around the delay.

A NVSD officer appeared near the entrance.

Not abruptly. Not announced. One moment the space held only volunteers and staff, and the next a figure occupied the doorway, posture relaxed, hands visible, presence unmistakable. Another followed a few minutes later and took up position near the wall.

They didn't approach the tables. They didn't speak. They didn't need to.

The standard shifted.

John felt it in the way people lowered their voices, in the way phones stayed pocketed, in the way movement became more deliberate. The room hadn't changed purpose, but its rules had.

The younger man stepped forward next. His identification was accepted and returned quickly. Relief crossed his face before he could stop it. He moved on, pulled into the interior of the building without looking back.

The third passenger advanced and was stopped at the first table. A brief exchange followed. Another request for documentation. A check that hadn't existed minutes earlier.

John registered the sequence as it unfolded, mapping cause and effect. He recognized the pattern forming, pulling against the plan he'd built on the drive over. The timing was the thing he hadn't accounted for.

The group was no longer whole.

The older woman remained at the secondary table, answering questions that seemed to circle without closing. The NVSD officer near the wall shifted his weight, attention fixed loosely in their direction.

John stayed where he was. He kept his hands visible. He resisted the urge to close the distance.

The friction held.

The older woman returned from the secondary table with her documents gathered back into the plastic folder, edges no longer aligned. She held it tighter now, one hand braced over the other, as if the papers might slip away if she loosened her grip.

She spoke quietly, leaning forward across the table. John couldn't hear the words. Polite. Explanatory. The way someone spoke when they believed respect and clarity would solve the problem.

She opened the folder again and slid something across the surface. Another document. Then another. She pointed once, just enough to guide attention. Her mouth kept moving softly.

The processor took the papers without looking up. Fingers moved faster now, less patient with the plastic sleeves. A glance at the screen. A longer look at one page. The processor's posture tightened, as if narrowing the interaction by inches.

The woman gestured lightly with one hand. A question, not a challenge.

The processor responded without lifting their head.

The woman paused. Tried again.

The processor's movements became more aggressive. Shorter exchanges. Fewer pauses. When the processor finally looked up, it was only to speak once, face flat, eyes already moving past her.

The woman's expression changed. Confusion tightening into something harder.

She stepped back half a pace, then stopped. Said something else, quieter now. Her hands moved to the folder again, thumbs worrying the worn edge.

The processor shook their head once. A sentence delivered at the same volume as everything else. No emphasis. No explanation offered.

The woman absorbed it slowly. She nodded, though nothing had been agreed to. She gathered her papers as if preparing to leave, then hesitated, glancing toward the entrance. She turned back, asked one more question.

The processor didn't answer this time.

She stood just beyond the table, close enough to remain visible, far enough not to obstruct anyone else. The folder stayed open in her hands, papers still arranged for review. She waited, eyes fixed on the processor, expecting a correction. A redirect. Another instruction.

The line moved around her.

John saw her shoulders rise and fall more quickly. Saw the way she shifted her weight and then stilled, as if afraid movement might count against her.

One of the NVSD officers appeared from behind a screen.

The look lingered on her for a moment longer than necessary. No gesture followed. No step forward. Just attention, measured and impersonal.

The woman noticed. Her spine straightened. She closed the folder at last and held it against her chest.

The processor was already engaged with the next person.

The system continued.

John stayed where he was, eyes moving between the woman and the table. He didn't hear the denial, but he knew it.

He felt the plan breaking on a rule set that no longer applied.

The woman remained standing just outside the line, documents pressed flat, worried.

The first NVSD officer approached the woman from her blind side.

He didn't rush. He didn't raise his voice. He stopped at an angle that blocked her view of the table without fully facing her, close enough to be unmistakable, far enough to avoid contact.

She looked up at him, confusion overtaking whatever patience she had left.

He spoke briefly. John couldn't hear the words, only the cadence. Flat. Directive.

The woman shook her head once, small and uncertain. She said something back, her mouth forming a question. She lifted the folder again, instinctively.

The second officer stepped in, mirroring the first.

They moved together then, hands settling on her arms just above the elbow. Practiced and firm.

The woman stiffened.

"Wait," she said, louder now. John heard that much. Her voice rose, not in volume but in pitch. "I don't understand. I didn't—"

They guided her away from the table.

The movement was smooth, efficient. She stumbled once, caught herself, and looked back over her shoulder toward the processor, then toward the entrance, searching for a reference point that no longer applied.

Fear arrived all at once.

Her breathing quickened. She clutched the folder tighter, knuckles whitening around the plastic edge. "Where are you taking me?" she asked. "I didn't do anything wrong."

The officers didn't answer.

They adjusted their grip and continued toward the exit.

John moved before he fully registered the decision.

"Hey," he said, stepping into their path just enough to be noticed. His hands stayed open, palms visible. His voice carried, but only as far as it needed to. "She's not causing a problem."

One of the officers turned his head toward John. The fabric covering his face shifted slightly as he did, lenses catching the overhead light. There was nothing to meet John's gaze but reflected movement.

"She has her paperwork," John added. "She just wants some clarification why she can't vote."

The officer facing him didn't respond immediately. His posture changed instead, weight redistributing, stance widening by inches.

"This doesn't involve you," he said at last.

John held his ground. He didn't step closer. He didn't reach out. He kept his hands where they were.

"She was asking a question," John said. "She's confused. That's all."

The officer's attention settled fully on him now, no expression to read, only alignment. Shoulders squared. Feet planted. A decision taking shape without announcement.

Behind them, the line continued to move.

The processor had already turned back to the screen. Another voter stepped forward. Papers changed hands. The room absorbed the disruption without breaking rhythm.

The woman let out a small sound, halfway between a breath and a plea. She twisted slightly, trying to look back at John as the officers steered her toward the doors.

"Please," she said, to no one in particular.

The officer closest to John lifted one hand, palm out.

"Step back."

The words were calm. Final.

John didn't touch him.

He didn't step forward either.

But he didn't step away.

The officers adjusted their positions, bodies angling to shield the woman as they moved. One of them glanced at the door, then back at John, recalculating.

John felt the room narrow around the moment. A few stopped to point their phones capturing the moment but most kept the line moving. People choosing to quietly protect themselves over confrontation.

He understood then that whatever happened next would no longer be administrative.

John stepped into their path as the officers shifted the woman toward the doors.

He didn't reach for them. Not exactly. He moved his body where theirs needed to go, an instinctive block, hands lifting as if to steady the moment rather than stop it.

The contact was brief. A forearm brushing a vest. Fabric against fabric.

That was enough.

"Back—" someone started.

The spray hit him mid-word.

His eyes slammed shut on reflex, but it was already everywhere. Fire across his face, his nose, his mouth. His breath caught hard in his chest, lungs seizing as if they'd been warned too late. He gagged and staggered, hands flying up, the world collapsing into white heat and noise.

"Down. Down now!"

Hands were on him immediately. Too many to track. Someone hooked his arm and twisted. Another hit the back of his knee. The floor came up fast, tile slamming into his shoulder as his weight went out from under him.

His face scraped sideways. The burn followed him there.

He tried to pull air and couldn't get enough of it. His chest was heavy, pinned. A knee drove down between his shoulder blades, then shifted higher, pressure settling just below his collarbone. Not crushing. Not careful. Enough to keep him where he was.

"Hands out!"

He coughed, spit stringing, eyes streaming uncontrollably. The pain made it hard to tell where his hands were. He dragged one forward anyway, palm scraping tile, fingers curling uselessly.

"I can't—" he tried, but the words drowned in the chemical burn.

"Hands! Now!"

The pressure on his chest didn't let up. His breath came in short, panicked pulls that never quite filled him.

Nearby, the woman screamed.

The sound cut through the noise, sharp and terrified. "Please—please—what are you doing? I didn't—please —"

Her voice broke. Someone spoke to her, low and fast, words stacked too close together to separate. She cried out again, closer now, then farther away as they moved her.

John tried to turn his head toward the sound. The knee pressed harder in response, forcing his face back down. The floor was cold against his cheek, slick with tears and saliva.

"Do not resist."

He wasn't. He couldn't.

Around him, the room kept moving. Shoes stepped around his body. A chair scraped and was repositioned. Someone cleared their throat and called the next voter forward.

"Next."

Papers moved. A pen scratched. The system reasserted its rhythm.

The pressure on his chest eased just enough for him to suck in a ragged breath. It burned all the way down. His vision flickered between brightness and shadow, shapes swimming at the edges.

The woman's voice faded toward the doors, her words dissolving into sound rather than meaning.

John lay there, restrained and gasping, cheek pressed to the tile, while the line advanced.

The polling place continued.

Early February 2029

They let him out through the front doors just after noon.

No explanation. No paperwork handed back beyond what he already had. The doors opened, and the building exhaled him into the light like a body it no longer needed to account for.

The cold arrived first. Not sharp, just persistent. It slid under his clothes and stayed there. He stood on the concrete for a moment, blinking, eyes watering from more than brightness. The world looked overexposed, edges too clean.

He was thinner. He felt it in the way his clothes hung, the extra length of belt folded back on itself, the hollow beneath his cheekbones when he caught his reflection in the glass doors behind him. His hands shook when he flexed them, a fine tremor that didn't stop when he clenched his fists. His skin looked pale, almost gray.

Noise pressed in from across the street.

A crowd had gathered along the sidewalk, spilling down the block. Cardboard signs bobbed above heads. A chant broke apart as it echoed off the buildings, voices answering out of sync. None of it was aimed at him. It was pressure venting wherever space allowed.

He took a step forward, limping with a new lasting pain that he would never truly recover from. He had to stop briefly to steady himself.

A woman detached from the edge of the crowd and crossed toward him, moving with the ease of someone who had done this many times before. No markings. No vest. A knit cap pulled low and a jacket that had seen better winters.

She stopped just short of him, eyes scanning his face, then gave a small nod toward the folding table set up near the curb.

A couple of people stood there with coolers and cardboard boxes. Sealed bottles of water were passed hand to hand. Someone shook out a blanket and folded it again when it didn't sit right.

She angled her body toward the curb and waited.

He followed.

Lowering himself down took more effort than he expected. The concrete bled cold through his pants. A bottle of water was pressed into his hands. He drank too fast and had to stop, coughing, chest hitching. No one commented. The pause was practiced.

A wrapped sandwich replaced the empty space in his lap. He stared at it for a moment before unwrapping it with clumsy fingers.

A blanket settled over his shoulders. It smelled faintly of detergent.

Nearby, the woman gestured toward the table, then toward the doors behind him, explaining something to another volunteer in a low voice. Her hands moved in short, efficient arcs. In and out. People came out. People needed a minute.

He ate slowly, jaw working harder than it should have. The protest noise rolled over them in uneven waves. Sirens sounded somewhere farther off, not close enough to matter.

A man crouched near the curb, checking his phone. He glanced up, thumb still hovering over the screen, and tipped the device toward the street. "Third Street. Same lot as before. "He didn't elaborate.

The woman acknowledged it with a brief nod, then shifted her attention back to John.

He looked up. "My car's there." The words scraped their way out, rough and underused.

Another nod. A hand lifted in a loose, encompassing gesture. That was already the plan.

They helped him up when he finished eating. The blanket stayed around his shoulders. As they walked toward a battered van parked down the block, he glanced back once at the building. The doors were already shut. The glass reflected the crowd instead of him.

The protest continued, indifferent.

The van door slid closed. Another bottle of water appeared beside him.

Something settled then. Not relief. Not calm. Just the understanding that the next phase had already started, whether he felt ready for it or not.

The van moved with traffic, neither fast nor slow. The city slid by in familiar layers, streets he knew by feel if not by recent memory. Storefronts. Bus stops. A stretch of road where the paint had never quite held.

The blanket stayed around his shoulders. He held the bottle of water loosely in one hand while angling his other toward the heating vent, fingers spread, soaking in the thin stream of warmth. Each swallow came easier than the last.

No one asked him questions.

The woman in the passenger seat watched the road ahead, one hand braced against the dash as the van took a shallow turn. In the back, someone adjusted a box at their feet to keep it from tipping. The movement was economical, practiced.

They passed another cluster of people gathered near an intersection. Not a protest this time. Just a knot of bodies, waiting. Someone handed out flyers. Someone else waved a sign that didn't match the others.

"Same thing everywhere," the man in back muttered, more to the window than to anyone else. "They keep locking folks up and then wondering why people protest."

No one contradicted him.

"Congress doesn't do anything," the woman up front added after a moment. Her tone stayed even, observational. "So much for checks and balances."

She shifted in her seat, eyes still on the road.

"People can't even leave," she continued. "Paperwork. Visas. Planes. Jackson is a dictator and congress just talks. And people that stand up get locked-up into some holding cell until they're just gone."

The van rolled through a green light and into the next block.

The sentence hung there, unfinished.

John watched the city move past the window. Warehouses gave way to chain-link, then to a stretch of road lined with palms that had been cut back to stubs. He thought about movement. About delays that didn't announce themselves. About time spent between points that never showed up on a map.

No one asked him what he thought.

John leaned forward slightly, eyes fixed ahead.

Something in his chest shifted. Not urgency. Alignment.

The gap had shape now.

The impound lot sat behind a chain-link fence topped with loops of wire that caught the light and held it. Rows of vehicles filled the space in orderly neglect, each one tagged, each one waiting for a reason to move again.

The van rolled to a stop near the office. An engine idled somewhere farther down the row, then cut out. The air smelled like oil, dust, and old heat.

Someone buzzed them through the gate.

John stepped out slowly. The blanket slid from his shoulders and was caught before it hit the ground, folded once, then set aside. The cold felt sharper here, unfiltered by walls or crowds. He drew a breath and let it settle where it could.

The Impala was three rows in, angled slightly out of line, paper tag taped inside the windshield. It hadn't been parked with care. Just dropped where the tow truck had left it.

Seeing it there landed differently than he expected.

Nothing about the car itself had changed.

The paint still held its dull sheen. No new dents. No broken glass. The tires looked the same as he remembered, pressure intact, posture patient. A second tag hung from the mirror, edges curled, ink already fading.

He crossed the distance without thinking about it.

The key turned stiffly in the lock. The door opened with the same familiar complaint. Inside, the air carried the smell of leather, a trace of some cleaner underneath. The quilt was still folded across the back seat, undisturbed.

John stood there for a moment, one hand on the doorframe.

Then he sat.

The seat adjusted to his weight with a soft shift. He pulled the door closed and rested his hands on the wheel. The cabin wrapped around him, narrow and private. The world outside the windshield felt suddenly distant, reduced to shapes and motion.

"What happened to it all?" His throat hurt saying those words. "I'm sorry Baby Girl it's all gone and I don't know if it's ever coming back." His heart hurt more.

He thought about borders that weren't marked. About delays that swallowed people whole. About how easy it was to stop someone from going forward without ever pushing them back.

Things moved all the time.

Cars. Packages. Information. People when no one was watching closely enough.

He reached up and touched the keychain, pink plastic knocking softly against the steering column as it settled. The letters were worn now, edges smoothed by handling.

BABY GIRL.

The engine turned over on the first try.

John sat with it idling, breath evening out, heat beginning to creep through the vents. Outside the fence, the city went on, unaware and untroubled by the gap he had just learned how to see.

He pulled the car into gear and drove out of the lot.

3

The Restoration

October sunlight spilled through the open garage door, turning dust into glitter and catching the steam rising from David's coffee. The '68 Impala sat half-skinned in the center of the space, a skeleton with ambition. John Anderson wiped his hands on a rag and studied the engine block they'd scrubbed clean enough to eat off.

"Looking good, Dad," Emily called from under the car.

Her voice came muffled, then she rolled out on a creeper with a streak of grease across her cheek and a socket wrench in her hand like it belonged there. At eighteen, she handled tools with the same confidence she'd learned surviving middle school, the year her mother left and the world stopped being predictable.

John tapped the fender. "Watch that brake line."

Emily flicked her eyes up, grinning. "Yes, sir."

David Torres set his mug on the workbench and ran his fingers along the engine's surface. "Clean as it's going to get. We can start rebuilding next weekend."

John smiled despite himself. Fifteen years of friendship had turned David into something like family. Not the easy kind, the real kind. The kind you could yell at and still hand a wrench to an hour later.

The radio on the bench coughed out campaign ads between classic rock songs.

''Restore our values''

'' Take back America''

''Protect real Americans''

Emily made a face. "Can we please change the station? If I hear one more guy threatening to save me from something I didn't ask for, I'm going to set the radio on fire."

John's jaw tightened. "You're voting age now, kiddo. Time to pay attention."

"I am paying attention," Emily said, wiping her hands on her jeans. "That's the problem."

David didn't look up. He kept his attention on the engine, on bolts and clean metal, on anything that didn't have a shouting man attached to it.

John picked up a wrench. "You decide what you're doing about that ballot?"

Emily's shoulders rose and fell once. "Still thinking."

"Not much to think about," John said, casual and certain. "One side's talking sense. The other side just wants to destroy our values."

David's eyes stayed on the engine. "Grocery costs are up. I'll give you that."

"Exactly," John said. "And my shop's getting squeezed. My guys are hurting."

Emily watched her father speak. The words sounded familiar, like something he'd said for years. But now they had a sharper edge, and she couldn't tell when it had grown.

The radio switched mercifully to "Sweet Home Alabama."

David nodded toward the engine. "Hand me the socket wrench. I think I found what's been knocking."

John passed it over, and for a while the garage returned to what it was supposed to be: tools, sweat, and the steady belief that anything broken could be taken apart and put back together if you cared enough.

David set the socket on a stubborn bolt and leaned in. The metal gave a tiny squeal, like it was offended to be asked.

"Easy," John warned. "You strip that, we'll be chasing threads all day."

David eased off, adjusted the angle, tried again. The bolt turned, grudging as a confession.

Emily leaned against the workbench and watched them work like she was memorizing the shape of the moment.

John told himself he was being practical.

That was the word he liked. Practical. Like replacing a capacitor before the whole unit fried. Like putting money away for emergencies. Like voting for the guy who said he would cut through the noise.

It did not feel like hate. It did not feel like cruelty.

It felt like keeping your head down and your family safe.

A couple Sundays later, First Baptist of Jacksonville smelled like hymnals, perfume, and old carpet cleaned too often with too little money. Emily sat beside her father and tried not to grind her teeth.

Pastor Richards stood under the cross. "Just as Jesus cleansed the temple," Richards thundered, "we must cleanse our nation of those who corrupt our children and undermine God's truth."

The congregation murmured amen like a reflex.

Emily glanced across the sanctuary. The Ramirez family sat a few rows ahead, stiff and quiet. Their kids used to run the aisles before service, laughing. Now they were still as statues.

Afterward, fellowship hour used to be tamales and sweet-and-sour meatballs and laughter in three languages. Now it was store cookies and weak coffee and a room arranged into invisible borders. People grouped and ungrouped with a kind of practiced choreography, like chairs being quietly moved while nobody admitted they'd touched them.

Emily started toward Mrs. Ramirez, but John caught her arm.

"Deacons' meeting," he said. "Come on."

"Dad, they've been leaving early every week."

"Later," he said, already steering her toward the conference room.

Inside, the deacons gathered around a table cluttered with voter guides mixed with prayer requests. Richards handed out pamphlets with a plastic smile.

"We need to be warriors," he said. "The enemy is not just out there. It's in our schools. In our libraries. In our children's minds."

Emily kept her mouth shut and stared at the pamphlet.

The enemy.

According to the guide, one of them was David.

John's voice joined the chorus like it belonged there.

When Emily looked up, she saw Deacon Harlan watching her the way he watched the offering plate. Measuring. Recording.

As they filed out, Harlan fell into step beside John.

"Good meeting," he said, voice warm as syrup. "Hard times call for clear eyes."

John nodded. "We have to protect what's ours."

Harlan's gaze drifted to Emily. "And our young people. Lots of— influences these days."

Emily felt the side-eye like a hand on the back of her neck.

On the bulletin board in the hallway, a new flyer sat pinned beside the church picnic notice.

Civic Duty Starts at Home.

A hotline number. A promise of anonymity. A smiling family beneath a flag.

Emily stared at it until the paper blurred.

John saw the flyer too.

He reached toward it without thinking, fingers hovering over the paper. Then he felt eyes on him. Harlan's. Richards's. The kind of attention that turned a man into a suspect.

John lowered his hand. "It's for criminals. For people who are troublemakers. For real threats—

Good people like us have nothing to worry about."

Election Night

The living room glowed blue from the TV. John sat forward in his recliner, remote in hand, while Emily scrolled results on her phone like she was looking for a way out.

"Florida's looking good," John said. "Turnout's strong."

Emily didn't look up. "Mrs. Ramirez got turned away. They told her one of her documents didn't match exactly."

John waved it off. "Rules are rules. If people want to vote, they should have their paperwork straight."

Emily stared at him, waiting for the line to soften into a joke. It didn't.

Her phone buzzed with a text from David.

I know your dad voted for Jackson. No matter what happens, you are both still family.

The anchor's voice sharpened. "CNA now calls the election. Senator Richard Jackson will be the next President of the United States."

The crowd on the screen erupted like a stadium. Jackson walked onstage with flags behind him and certainty in his posture.

"My fellow Americans," he said. "Tonight, we restore our values. Tonight, we take back our country. Tonight, we decide who the real Americans are."

John stood up like he was in church. He cheered.

Emily's throat tightened. She watched her father's face, flushed with relief and pride, like he'd been waiting years for this.

"This is it, kiddo," he said. "Things are finally going to change."

"Yeah, Dad," Emily whispered.

They really were.

Two weeks after the inauguration

A cold snap rolled through Jacksonville like it didn't belong there. The garage smelled of coffee and machine oil. John and David hunched over the engine compartment while Emily sat cross-legged on the workbench with her phone and a mug that didn't warm her hands enough.

David had brought a cardboard box this time. He set it down like it was heavier than it looked.

"What's that?" John asked, then immediately wished he hadn't. The question sounded like more than curiosity. It sounded nosy.

David peeled the tape with his thumbnail. Inside were books, spines outward. A couple had bright stickers slapped across the covers. The stickers left a tacky residue when he tried to lift one.

"School," David said. Just that.

Emily slid off the bench, leaned in, and read one of the sticker labels upside down. Her mouth tightened.

John stared at the box. "You moving classrooms?"

David kept his eyes on a sticker that said 'BANNED'. He worked it free, slow and careful. The cover underneath came away with it in a thin torn layer, like skin.

"They told me to get rid of these," he said. "I thought Emily might like some of them."

John frowned. "Get rid of them? Why?"

David didn't answer right away. He set the sticker aside on a scrap of paper like it was a bug he didn't want to touch.

"New regulations," he said finally. "Came down from the new board of Ed."

Emily's phone buzzed. She glanced down, then tucked it under her thigh like she could smother it. "They're doing it everywhere," she said.

John winced as if she was complaining. "Not all books are for all kids. Maybe being more selective is a good thing."

David leaned over the engine and tightened a bolt. The wrench slipped. The sound echoed off the garage walls, sharp as a snapped promise.

"Damn," David muttered, then softer, "sorry."

"Don't worry about it." John responded in a friendly tone, "It's fine." But he knew better. "Just remember that rounded edges happen one quarter-turn at a time."

David wiped his hands. "Can we get back to the car?"

John nodded too quickly.

They worked on the Impala in silence for a while. John set a gasket in place, the rubber stiff from age. He pressed it down anyway. "It'll hold. It has to. New ones are expensive and last time I ordered they sent me an email full of apologies about back orders and no idea when the order was going to be filled."

Emily watched the gasket, then watched her father's face.

"Dad," she said quietly, "you're forcing it."

John's jaw tightened. "It's fine."

David didn't look up. "That's what everybody says right before it leaks."

John let out a sharp breath. "Don't start."

Tools clinked. Silence thickened.

"Stop overreacting," John picked up a tool. "You two always think things are worse than they are."

That was another story John liked. A familiar one. It made the world simpler.

It let him keep the garage as a sanctuary.

It let him keep David.

Spring came with pollen on everything, even the Impala's bare metal, a fine yellow dust that made the car look sick. John kept a towel by the sink now, not for hands but for wiping the workbench clean before the grit could get into anything important.

At the shop, Jorge waited in the office before opening, hands clasped like he was holding himself together.

"I have to quit," he said. His eyes stayed on the floor. "They sent a letter. It's about my grandmother's paperwork. They want me to come in for a review, and my cousin says…"

He swallowed.

John sat down hard in his office chair. "Jorge, you were born here."

Jorge's laugh was small and humorless. "That used to mean something."

John offered to call someone, to talk to someone, to fix it the way he fixed air conditioners. Jorge shook his head.

"My cousin waited too long in Arizona," he said. "They took the house. The savings. The kids went to a 'youth facility' while they verified status. Nobody's seen them since."

After Jorge left, John threw himself into work, because work made sense. Work had rules. You diagnose, you repair, you replace. You restore.

The next Sunday, Deacon Harlan caught him by the fellowship hall doors before John could slip out.

"John," Harlan said, smiling like a man who expected obedience, "Richards is putting together a prayer list. Folks worried about… disruptions."

"Disruptions?" John asked.

Harlan's smile tightened. "People with agendas. People who use medical stuff as a weapon. People who teach children to doubt."

His gaze slid toward the hallway, toward the youth room, toward the world where Emily existed.

John felt a cold pressure behind his ribs.

"We're just trying to live," John said.

"Exactly," Harlan replied. "So we watch. We stay alert. We do our part."

John hesitated a moment. Then nodded.

By the time the cicadas started up, the garage had turned into a kiln. John's shirt clung to his back. David wiped sweat from his forehead and leaned into the engine compartment like he could muscle the Impala back to life by force of will.

Emily sat on the bench, phone in hand, eyes flicking between the screen and her father.

"Try it," David called.

John turned the key. The engine coughed, sputtered, and died.

"Damn it," John muttered.

Emily made a sharp sound. Both men turned.

Her face had gone pale. "It's the Ramirez family," she said, voice shaking. "They took them. All of them."

David straightened slowly. "What do you mean, took them?"

Emily's fingers flew over her phone. "Maria posted. They came at dawn. Said Carlos's citizenship was under review because of his grandmother's paperwork."

John stared at her like the words were in another language. "Carlos was born here. His kids were born here. He pays taxes. He coaches Little League."

David's voice stayed quiet, but it cut. "My parents paid taxes for thirty years before they got citizenship."

John's head snapped toward him. "What?"

David didn't look up. "Last week at Publix someone told me to go back where I came from."

John's mouth opened. Closed. Opened again. Nothing came out that wasn't useless.

Emily's phone buzzed again. "They're taking them to Camp Roosevelt," she said. "That 'processing facility' out by the base."

David echoed the phrase like it tasted bad. 'Processing facility.'

John grabbed a wrench because he needed something solid to hold. "There has to be a reason. They don't just…"

Emily's voice cracked. "Dad, they just did."

John stared at the open hood, at metal and grease and the thing he could fix if he tried hard enough.

"This isn't what I voted for," he said.

David finally looked at him. His eyes were tired and steady. "It is. You just thought it would stop before it got to us."

Emily's tone softened, and that made it worse. "When they said 'take back America,' who did you think they were taking it from?"

John swallowed hard. His grip on the wrench tightened until his knuckles burned.

David spoke like he was tired down to the bone. "Carlos told me last month he was grateful his grandmother wasn't alive to see this. At least she died believing the dream was real."

John's throat closed.

"What can we do?" he asked, and it sounded like the first honest thing he'd said in months.

Emily glanced at David, then back to John. "They're letting church members bring clothes," she said carefully. "Visit. Maybe…"

John nodded reflexively. "Yeah. Yeah, we'll go."

He didn't know what he thought he could do. Apologize to a whole camp. Negotiate with a system.

Restore something.

That night, John lay in bed and listened to the house settle.

He thought about Carlos coaching Little League.

He thought about the flyer in the church hallway.

He thought about the word "processing," and the way it turned people into paperwork.

He told himself there would be hearings, judges, a reason.

Then he caught himself.

He realized he had been telling himself stories for months.

Winter came again, and the space heater in the garage worked like it was tired. John flipped through a parts catalog and felt his stomach drop at the prices.

David whistled low. "If you can even find them."

John set the catalog down and rubbed his thumb across an old grease stain on the page. It felt like a bruise.

Emily had moved back home after her scholarship stopped stretching far enough. She sat with her laptop open, community college tabs in one window, news alerts in another. She didn't read them so much as brace against them.

John's phone buzzed with another supplier cancellation. Third this week. He'd laid off two mechanics, good men with kids, men who'd cheered on TV right alongside him.

Outside, a military convoy rumbled past.

John met David's eyes this time. Didn't look away.

"So," Emily said, voice low, "what are we going to do about it?"

John glanced at the Impala. At the pieces. At the work. At the way they'd learned to reuse what should've been replaced.

"We start with what we can fix," he said. "Then we work our way up."

It sounded brave.

It also sounded too late.

By the time the days started stretching again, James showed up at sunset in a Civic that sounded like it was holding its organs in with duct tape. David winced at the idle.

"That's James," he said. "Timing's shot."

James stepped into the garage still in his scrubs, tired but smiling when he saw them. He carried a paper bag.

"Dumplings," he announced. "Mrs. Chen sent them."

Emily grinned, and for a moment the garage felt like it used to.

John offered to install a smart thermostat to cut their electric bill. It was a small act, almost domestic, a way to insist they were still the same people.

James smiled, but there was strain under it. "Board wants extra documentation," he said quietly. "More forms. More questions."

John frowned. "About what?"

James shrugged, and the shrug was too practiced. "Everything."

John heard the word and felt his stomach go tight. Everything was the kind of thing you couldn't fix with a wrench.

James's gaze stayed gentle and exhausted. "They can do whatever they want, John. No one is stopping them."

Emily watched her father absorb that, watched the old certainty falter and try to stand back up.

It did. It always did.

Late summer came back heavy, the air humming with cicadas as David made final adjustments to the carburetor. John sat ready in the driver's seat while Emily perched on her usual workbench, all of them holding their breath. Two years of scrounging parts, of makeshift repairs, of hoping; it all came down to this moment.

"Okay," David said, stepping back. "Try it now."

John turned the key. The engine coughed once, twice, then roared to life. The sound was perfect, a deep, healthy rumble that echoed off the garage walls. For a moment, none of them moved, as if afraid any sudden motion might break the spell.

Then Emily whooped, jumping down from her perch. "You did it! You actually did it!"

"No, we did it," David corrected, grinning as he wiped his hands. "All of us."

John revved the engine slightly, his face glowing with pride. The Impala responded smoothly, purring like it had just rolled off the assembly line. He cut the engine and got out, running his hand along the car's frame.

"Never thought we'd see her running again," he said softly. "Not with everything..."

"Calls for a celebration," David said, reaching into a cooler. He pulled out three bottles of his home-brewed porter, a luxury these days, with commercial beer prices through the roof. "Been saving these for a special occasion."

They settled into their usual spots: John on an old lawn chair, David leaning against the workbench, Emily cross-legged on top of it. The garage felt different somehow, warmer, more like home than it had in months.

"To the Impala," David said, raising his bottle. "And to family."

They clinked bottles. Emily barely wet her lips, then set the bottle down too carefully.

David watched her. John watched her too, the way fathers learned to watch when they'd been the only parent for long enough.

"So," David said during a lull, keeping his tone casual, "how's that new boyfriend of yours? Jason, right? Haven't heard you mention him lately."

Emily's smile broke. She put both hands flat on the workbench like she needed the support.

"Emily?" John started to rise, worry sharp on his face.

"I'm sorry," she whispered. "I'm so sorry, Dad. I... I'm pregnant."

The garage went silent except for the tick of the cooling engine. John sank back into his chair, his face blank for a beat, like his mind had stepped out of his body.

"Jason," he said finally, voice tight. "He knows?"

Emily nodded. "He left. Said he couldn't afford a baby, said it was my fault and my problem. He said he's moving north to try to find work."

John's hands clenched into fists. Rage flashed, then folded in on itself.

David stepped forward. "Does anyone else know?"

"Just Maria." Emily's voice cracked as she wiped her eyes. "She helped me find a clinic, but... Dad, I can't... I want to keep it. Even with everything so messed up, I want..."

"Of course you're keeping it," John said, voice rough with emotion. He stood and crossed to his daughter, pulling her into a tight hug. "We'll figure it out. Together."

"You know," Emily said, voice small but trying for normal, "I always thought it was funny how you two act like you don't need anybody."

John sniffed, wiping his face with the back of his hand. "We're fine."

"Sure," Emily said. "Two grown men, one car, and a whole lot of denial."

David groaned. "Here we go."

Emily's eyes lit the way they did when she talked about horror like it was a second language.

David pinched the bridge of his nose. "Please don't."

Emily grinned and did it anyway, sing-song and affectionate.

"One of us. One of us."

John rolled his eyes, but a laugh slipped out, uninvited.

Emily added, quieter, like a charm. "You're one of us. Gooble gabble, you are one of us!" John snorted.

For a moment the garage warmed, not from the heater, but from the stubborn refusal to let the world take this too.

Sunday dinner at David and James's place smelled like fresh bread and herbs. It had become their ritual of normalcy, even if the menu was simpler these days.

Emily had started a garden in the spring with James's patient guidance. Tonight's salad came from the backyard. The basil looked like a small miracle.

"That basil's looking good," James said, peering over her shoulder at the herbs she was chopping. His hands were precise as he sliced tomatoes, each movement efficient from years of practice. Despite the gray touching his temples, his dark eyes were warm behind his glasses. "Told you that corner spot would get the right amount of sun."

"Yeah, yeah, you're always right," Emily teased. "Must be exhausting, being perfect all the time."

"Oh, it is," James said, grinning. "Just ask David."

"Stop inflating his ego," David called from the living room where he and John were setting the table. "His head's big enough already."

They fell into the rhythm of passing dishes and sharing stories. James talked about his practice, packed to the doors. David mentioned former students who still kept in touch, then stopped mid-sentence and smiled like he'd bitten his tongue.

John updated them on the shop. Still struggling, but surviving.

Emily was quieter than usual. John noticed her hand tremble when she reached for her water glass. She barely touched her food.

"Emily?" he asked softly. "Everything okay?"

Emily set down her fork. Her face had gone pale in a way that had nothing to do with nerves. "I... I had some pain yesterday. And this morning. There's... there's something wrong."

John straightened. "What kind of pain? Where?"

"Sharp," Emily whispered. "Lower right side. And there was bleeding."

James reached across the table and covered her hand with his. "Do you want me to tell them?"

Emily nodded, eyes wet.

"She called me yesterday," James said, meeting David and John's looks. "I got her in for an ultrasound."

John's shoulders sagged in relief for a breath. Ultrasound. Clinic. Fixable.

Then James inhaled like the air had weight.

"It's ectopic," he said.

The word dropped into the room and did not bounce.

John's fork clattered against his plate. "What does that mean? Is she going to be okay?"

James chose his words carefully. "It can't survive. And it can kill her if we wait." Emily's grip tightened on James's hand.

"So you fix it," John said, voice rising. "You do whatever you need to do."

James and David exchanged a look.

James's voice went quieter. "It's not safe to do it here."

John blinked. "This is a medical emergency."

"It is," James said. "And the safest way to keep her alive is to leave the state."

John stared, not understanding, like language had betrayed him.

"There's a clinic up north," James said. "They can treat it quickly."

"Up north," John repeated, the words tasting like distance. "That's... that's a long drive."

David's jaw tightened. "And people get nosy about long drives now."

James nodded once. "The clinic can write it up like a consultation. It might help if we get questioned."

John heard the phrase get questioned and felt something hard and cold bloom behind his ribs.

"Insurance won't cover it," James added. "Not out of state."

"We've got savings," David said.

"And I can sell tools from the shop," John added immediately. A solution. A fix. Something he could do with his hands.

Emily's voice broke. "I can't ask y'all to do this. The penalties if we're caught…"

"You're not asking," John said. "We're telling."

David nodded once. "When do we leave?"

They spent the next hour planning: James listing symptoms that meant go now, David mapping routes on paper because he didn't trust a phone to keep a secret, John calculating money and what he could sell quickly.

The remains of dinner grew cold.

At one point, James went to the kitchen to rinse a plate, and John followed him.

"James," John whispered, low, like the house itself was listening. "If you do this, they'll come for you."

James stared at the water running over his hands. "They've been coming. They just call it reviews and paperwork."

John swallowed. "And you're still doing it."

James turned. His eyes were tired and furious and kind. "I took an oath. I'm done playing it safe while people suffer."

Two nights later, John sat in his truck outside his shop and stared at the dark windows. The streetlight above the lot flickered, buzzing like it couldn't decide whether it wanted to stay on.

He had parked there out of habit, like the building could give him answers if he sat close enough.

His hands smelled like metal and oil. His mouth still tasted like cold coffee. He stared at the shop sign, at his own name, and felt a strange distance from it. Like it belonged to a man who believed in rules.

He rested his forehead against the steering wheel.

"Lord," he said, and his voice surprised him with how thin it sounded.

He waited for the comfort that used to come with saying that word. Nothing came. The cab stayed the same temperature. The air stayed the same stale.

"Lord, I don't know how to talk to You anymore," he whispered. "I don't even know if I'm doing it right."

He laughed once, a small ugly sound. "I'm John Anderson. I fix air conditioners. I rebuild engines. I pay my taxes. I show up on Sundays. I did everything I was told was right."

He swallowed and felt the swallow scrape.

"I voted. I cheered. I clapped like it was a damn football game. I told myself I was being practical. I told myself I was protecting my kid."

He squeezed his eyes shut and saw the church hallway. The flyer. Civic Duty Starts at Home. The hotline number. His hand hovering, then dropping away.

"I walked past it," he said. "I walked past it because I didn't want anyone looking at me."

Silence.

He breathed in, and the breath shook.

"Emily's in pain," he said, like he was reporting it to a dispatcher. "She keeps trying to smile. She keeps trying to make jokes like she's not scared. Like I'm not scared."

His voice thickened.

"Please don't take her," he said. "Please."

The words came out fast, then faster, as if he could outrun what he was asking.

"I know You don't bargain. I know You're not a vending machine. I know I'm not supposed to talk like this. But I don't know what else to do."

He wiped his face with the back of his hand, angry at the wetness like it had betrayed him.

"David and James," he whispered. "Keep them safe. They're good men. Better men than me. They've been trying to do the right thing while I've been... while I've been telling myself stories."

He stared into the windshield and imagined Emily in a hospital bed while someone explained things in a calm voice, like calm was the same as help.

He imagined a doctor shrugging, hands helpless, eyes apologetic.

He imagined himself nodding, because he had been trained to nod.

"No," he said. "No. Not this time."

His hands tightened around the steering wheel.

"If You have to take somebody," he said, voice breaking, "take me. Take my shop. Take my pride. Take whatever You want, just leave her here. I'll trade. I will. I'll do it gladly."

The cab stayed quiet.

The streetlight buzzed.

John waited anyway, because hope was a habit. Because prayer was the last tool he had left and he did not know how to hold it without breaking it.

When nothing answered, he whispered, smaller, like he was talking to a sleeping child.

"I'm sorry," he said. "I'm sorry I waited until it was my daughter."

He sat there until the flicker of the streetlight steadied, and he could pretend that meant something.

The next two days felt like a blur of ordinary tasks turned into contraband.

John sold a compressor, a set of specialty gauges, and a tool chest he'd bought in better times. He told himself he could replace them later.

Emily packed a small bag and tried to make jokes. She watched her father in a way that made him feel exposed.

David printed maps on paper because he did not trust apps anymore. Not with how easily a phone could become a witness.

James filed clinic notes in a way that would look clean if someone audited him. He deleted texts after reading them. He stopped wearing his white coat outside.

At church, Pastor Richards preached about sacrifice.

"We are called to endure," he said. "We are called to resist temptation, and the temptation today comes wrapped in compassion."

Emily sat stiff beside John.

Deacon Harlan looked at her, then at James's hands, then at David, and smiled. "Hmm…"

After service, Harlan approached John.

"Heard James has been busy," he said lightly.

John's throat tightened. "He's a doctor."

"Of course," Harlan said. "Just... careful. People are talking. Folks don't want trouble."

John's pulse thudded in his ears.

Emily's fingers curled around his forearm.

"Thanks for your concern," John said, and hated the way it sounded like obedience.

Tuesday

They left before dawn.

The Impala's engine purred as they eased out of the driveway, its restored strength carrying them through the dark. John drove. David rode shotgun, phone dark, paper maps in his lap.

In the back seat, Emily lay with her head in James's lap while he monitored her breathing and checked her pulse with fingers gentle as prayer.

"How's the pain?" James asked.

"Manageable," Emily whispered, though her face was pale. "Just keep talking. It helps."

"Remember when you started that garden?" James said, trying to keep his voice steady. "You killed three tomato plants in the first week."

"Your fault," Emily managed a weak smile. "Should've warned me about overwatering."

"Had to let you learn," James said.

David glanced back, and his smile was tight but real. "You learned how to grow things. That's no small thing. That's real."

John's knuckles were white on the wheel. The Impala sounded too loud in the quiet, each rumble a declaration.

As the horizon lightened, John saw a billboard by the roadside.

REPORT SUSPICIOUS TRAVEL. PROTECT OUR COMMUNITIES.

A flag. A hotline. The same number from the church hallway.

John felt his stomach twist.

"Dad?" Emily whispered.

"I'm here," John said. "I'm right here."

He kept driving.

The county line came up fast.

Red and blue lights flared in the rearview mirror.

David's voice went flat. "Sheriff. Single car."

"Stay calm," James said. "We've got our story."

John pulled over. The Impala's engine ticked as it idled.

Two deputies approached, one on each side, flashlights sweeping across the interior.

"License and registration," said the deputy at John's window. His nameplate read Collins.

The second officer fidgeted with the gold band on his ring finger as he scanned the car.

John handed over his documents with hands that tried to look steady.

"Where you headed?" Collins asked.

"Visiting family in Georgia," John said.

"At four in the morning," Collins said, like the truth was obvious and ugly.

His flashlight swept the back seat, landing on Emily's pale face.

"What's wrong with her?"

"Carsick," James said quickly. "I'm a doctor. She's not feeling well."

"Doctor?" Collins's partner snapped his light to James's face. "Let me see ID."

James reached slowly for his wallet.

Collins walked back to the cruiser with the documents. The second deputy stayed at the passenger side, hand hovering near his holster like a habit.

The minutes stretched.

A radio squawked from the cruiser, thin and crackling.

Collins returned with a different posture. Not bored now. Alert. Interested.

He handed John's license back like it was dirty.

"Step out of the vehicle," Collins said.

John blinked. "Is there a problem, officer?"

"Step out," Collins repeated, louder. "Now."

James leaned forward, voice controlled. "Officer, she's unwell. We're trying to get her to a clinic."

Collins's eyes flicked to James, then to David, then back to Emily.

"We got a report," Collins said. "Suspicious travel. Medical."

John's stomach dropped.

David's voice was steady, careful. "A report from who?"

Collins smiled without humor. "Doesn't matter."

Emily made a small broken sound from the back seat. She doubled over, sharp and involuntary.

"Uncle James," she choked out. "Something's wrong."

James's face drained. "She's crashing. It may have ruptured."

He lunged for his medical bag.

"Don't move," the second deputy snarled, grabbing his arm. "Nobody's going anywhere until we figure out what's really going on here."

"She needs help," James said, pulling, urgency cracking through his control. "She's bleeding internally."

Collins yanked open John's door and dragged him out.

"Out of the car," Collins barked. "All of you. Now."

"Please," John said, the word raw. "My daughter's dying."

Collins looked into the car again, light flicking over David, over James, over Emily.

His mouth curled.

"Whole damn traveling freak show," he said.

The second deputy laughed once, short and mean.

Emily whimpered.

James tried to move toward her.

The deputy slammed him against the car.

David stepped forward on instinct. "Hey. Back off."

The baton came up.

Then everything went sideways.

The shot cracked across the empty highway.

David staggered, red blooming across his chest.

James made a sound that did not belong in a human throat.

"David!"

James caught his husband as he fell, cradling him close. "No. No, please, baby, stay with me."

"Freaks," Collins's partner spat, and kicked James in the ribs. "Should've known."

John tried to run back to the car.

Collins hit him in the mouth with the butt of his flashlight.

Stars exploded behind John's eyes.

He stumbled, tasted blood, heard Emily scream from inside the Impala.

He saw James on the ground, hands up, begging.

He saw David's eyes go unfocused.

He saw a country he could not fix.

John crawled back into the car, past the open door, past the cold air, into Emily's space.

She was shaking.

"Daddy," she whispered. "I'm cold."

"I'm here," John said, voice breaking. He pulled her close, pressing his cheek to her hair, trying to be a wall against the world. "I'm here, baby girl."

Outside, James's pleas turned into broken sobs.

The Impala's engine ticked as it cooled, each sound a clock. Leather seats staining red.

Emily's hand loosened in his, like she had finally stopped gripping the world.

"I'm sorry," John whispered, tears falling into her hair. "This is my fault. I thought... I thought I was keeping you safe."

About the Author

Karl Otto writes horror and dark speculative fiction exploring the strange edges of reality and the people who find themselves there.

His stories blend folklore, cosmic horror, and social unease, often asking uncomfortable questions about the world we live in.

When he isn't writing, he can usually be found drinking too much coffee, arguing with the internet, or working on the next unsettling story.

Thanks for reading.